MOVALWAR

BENJAMIN R CORNELIUS

First Published and printed in Great Britain in 2020 by Eklegein Ltd.

Cover design by Ben Cornelius

ISBN 978-1-90797-165-5
Eklegein Ltd
030920

Contents

Chapter One

The Beginning of The End

The ground sank as Mendoviolent walked his evil world, with pained wailing from the ground below and screaming in the sky. He was the new king of Movalwar. Movalwar is a hidden kingdom of pain and suffering. Once this land was full of hope and light and most of all freedom, but since Mendoviolent came to this world, he used an uncontrollable power named 'The Switch' - an orb that could only be controlled using a special gem. The Switch had the power to change the way you think forever. It had the power to change environments entirely.

Now remember when I said Movalwar was a hidden kingdom, right? Well, in a secret lake, legends tell of a gateway into this forgotten land, and the last people to fail in search of it were in the city of London. That's where our story begins.

* * *

Alfie was moping around his living room at home with nothing to do, simply bored. But just then he remembered 'Really Fast Racing Whippets' was on at 4 o'clock, it was his new favorite show. He rapidly ran into the kitchen where his mother - Linda, and Father - Will, were having another argument over what to eat.

"The fish will be nice," Dad said, with his head in the fridge.

"It's not even in date. It went out of date two days ago," Mum sighed. *"Throw it away!"*

"Alright, what about a chicken curry?" Dad suggested.

"Will, it feels like we have had curry our entire lives!" Mum moaned.

Alfie didn't have time for any more arguments; he needed to see what time it was, only to see that the clock read 3 o'clock. Urgh, another hour to wait.

Alfie let out a sigh of disbelief as he went up to his room not entirely knowing what he wanted to do when he got to the top of the stairs but Alfie was good at making fun when there was none to be had, and decided to play with his army action figures.

He had collected them all. It started out as a gift from Dad. It was a special memory he had not forgotten, undoing the wrapping paper and seeing Captain Major in the bright red box. Ever since then, he had saved up his money and he had slowly collected them all. Still to this day he plays with them - creating adventures and missions, ordering the troops and giving plan strategies.

Just as the German troops were about to raid the laundry basket, his phone started to ring. It was Bobby, his best friend. They'd become best friends since Bobby moved to Alfie's school two summers ago; they also took the same after-school clubs and sports training.

"Hi Buddy," said Bobby.

"Hey!"

"I have rung to tell you some awesome news!"

NEWS?! ... This is just what Alfie needed to cure the boredom. He listened intently.

"So... ya' know Trevor?" Alfie let out a sigh.

"Yeah... Unfortunately," he replied

Trevor was a school bully that used to bully Alfie for no particular reason at all. It had seemed to stop now that Alfie was hanging around with Bobby. Bobby explained that over the past week or so, Trevor had come down with something. Some sort of flu. He had been rushed to hospital, but nobody knows why. Alfie was secretly quite glad that he wasn't around but was intrigued as to why he was in the hospital with only flu symptoms.

Bobby said, *"My Mum said there is no school tomorrow because nobody wants to catch whatever it is that he has."*

Alfie was about to cheer when Mum shouted up the stairs, *"ALFIE! TEA, HUN."*

In the end they had curry and whilst Alfie sat there, he noticed the TV in the background. A reporter came on, speaking about some sort of virus where people get flu symptoms. It said that people were being urged to go to hospital immediately. Then it stopped, mid-sentence. Mum had swiped the remote and switched it off.

There was an eerie silence as they all ate... as if

something was going on…

Chapter Two

A Midnight Disturbance

B ut Alfie tried to just ignore it and eat his curry. Mum was right - it really did feel as if they had lived on curry their entire lives. He used to savour the sweet and sourness of the sauce and happily chew on the chicken. But he got used to the taste and eventually got sick of it.

The silence was suddenly broken by Dad's question, *"How's everybody's day today?"* That's when Alfie decided to mention it.

"Dad?"

"Yes, son,"

"Is there no more school?"

"NO MORE SCHOOL?" bellowed Dad.

"SCHOOL? YES, YES THERE IS SCHOOL YOUNG MAN!"

"Well … " he reasoned.

"DON'T 'WELL' ME, WHERE DID YOU GET THIS NONSENSE FROM?"

"Will, calm down!" Mum whispered.

Mum always told him to calm down. Alfie's Dad was the sort of person that would irrationally jump to conclusions, and get irritated over really little things and sometimes nothing at all.

"It's... just that... well... Bobby," Alfie started. Dad interrupted.

"THAT BOBBY IS NOTHING BUT A LOAD OF STINKING LIES, MY BOY!"

He knew it was no good trying to reason with him and ate the last of his curry. Then he heard Mum say, *"Alfie, can you just go into the living room or play some games for a while."*

"Why?" He asked impatiently.

"Alfie, just do what I say!" was the reply he got back from her.

After what felt like an eternity but was probably just an hour, Mum and Dad came through to the living room and confessed, *"Alfie, we have kept this a secret from you now for a few weeks but you need to go and stay at Granny Net-Net's for a few days, so I've packed you a..."*

He decided to stop her right there and ask a simple question ...

"But why, what's going on?"

"Because me and your father are going to the hospital to have a few tests; there's nothing to be worried about."

On the way to Granny's, the air was silent. No one spoke, as if there was a secret that nobody had told him about. Confused, Alfie stepped out of the car when they arrived at Granny's.

"Remember, we're going to be in the hospital for a couple of days, but we will ring you shortly; bye Sweetie." So Alfie said bye to Mum and Dad and hello to Granny and Grandad.

Alfie stayed up late and had lots of fun to take his mind off things. They played lots of scrabble (that he didn't really mind playing), saw a movie and looked at lots of photos of when Alfie was a baby, mentioning all the funny moments he had had in his early years. Alfie asked if his parents were going to be alright, and Granny was very adamant that they would be before changing the topic quickly, saying it was time for bed.

Alfie climbed into bed and looked around his bedroom.

"This is where you will be sleeping, Dear - do you like it?"

It was nice but would never feel like home.

"Night, night," whispered Granny.

"Goodnight," he said.

Slowly Alfie drifted off to sleep.

It was the middle of the night and Alfie was dreaming. The world was sleeping. And as he was dreaming, it felt as if something was at the back of his mind, something was trying to tell him something... SOMETHING was speaking...

He sensed that it wanted to speak to him, so he let it.

"YOU WILL GIVE ME WHAT I NEED," it said all of a sudden.

His head felt super heavy and rush after rush of headaches began to speed around his mind.

"YOU HAVE SOMETHING I NEED, GIVE ME IT BACK." His head started to throb.

It hurt every bone in his body.

"YOU SHALL COME TO MOVALWAR THROUGH THE SECRET LAKE AND YOU SHALL GIVE ME BACK MY POSSESSION SO I CAN CONTROL THE SWITCH AND ENSURE THAT MY KINGDOM STAYS DARK AND EVIL FOREVER!!!" ... and then it was gone.

* * *

Meanwhile ... in Movalwar

"I have sent the message; he shall give me back the gemstone so I can destroy it once and for all."

"NO ONE WILL EVER CHANGE THESE LANDS BACK TO LIGHT AND HOPE AGAIN!"

Chapter Three

Disease

Alfie woke up the next day wondering if that voice that spoke to him was in his imagination or had come from the shadows in his room; he ignored it and went downstairs.

"Hi, are you ok?" Alfie questioned

"I'm fine. What would you like for breakfast - toast or cornflakes?"

"Cornflakes, please."

Alfie sat at the old, rickety table and ate his cornflakes. When he asked if there were any more board games in the house, Granny said that there were some more in the attic.

So, Alfie searched for the step ladder and clambered into the attic. It was slightly damp, fusty and ever so cold; it wasn't the place he would dream of being but if there was another game besides scrabble, he'd do anything to get his hands on it. It turned out in fact that there weren't any board games that he could see and as he was about to give up and climb back down the ladder, something caught his eye.

It appeared to be a box with a silver plaque. Due to its peculiar shine, unlike the other boxes in the attic, Alfie was very drawn to the thought of opening it. He carefully undid the latches and lifted the lid to find a multi-coloured gemstone. It appeared to be a pearl or even a gem. Fascinated by such a rare and valuable object he decided to let greed get the better of him and keep the gemstone. And at that very instant he remembered the voice in his head asking for something; perhaps if the voice in his head was real it was asking for this.

Just as he was considering keeping it and not telling anybody, Granny shouted up

"ALFIE, YOUR MUM IS CALLING TO CHECK ON YOU, DEAR!"

"COMING!" shouted Alfie.

He put the gem in his brown jacket pocket and climbed down the stairs.

On the phone, Mum explained that she was fine and so was Dad. They told Alfie that there was a virus going about the town, and Mum and Dad went to have tests to see if they had the virus. The doctors said that they were both fine but they still had to stay in hospital for a few more days to make sure that they both didn't have it.

Later that night after having a nice, warm, succulent roast dinner Alfie's mobile phone started to ring; it was Bobby.

He decided to answer the phone but not tell Bobby about the gem in his pocket as he didn't want him to get jealous.

The pair talked and talked until Bobby had explained that Trevor's illness had become worse, and he was refusing to eat his food and his illness was now classed as:

'Cure not yet found',

'Danger level CRITICAL'.

Will Trevor survive??

Chapter Four

Magic

At first Alfie didn't believe what he was hearing, but after a bit more convincing information from Bobby, Alfie soon believed it. He was happy that Trevor wasn't attending school because he wouldn't be bullied anymore, but everyone thought he just didn't feel well and now as he thought more and more about it that night, the more and more it became true.

That night as he was walking upstairs, as it was time for bed, he suddenly remembered the gemstone in his jacket. So as he climbed into bed, he put it on the windowsill, and slowly drifted off to sleep. He was thinking about the past couple of days. All of it was a bit strange. The voice - if it was real. The gem from the attic. It all didn't seem right, and the last thing he could think about was what would happen next, before the land of sleep whisked him away.

It had been almost three hours since he fell asleep and something, somewhere, in his bedroom was happening right under his nose! The gemstone that he placed on the windowsill had started to glow. This array of wild lights woke Alfie, and he was astonished by what he had found. Just then the colours started to split and fly around the room in spectacular bursts. And then they all came together to show a map. There were mountains, islands, seas and jungles.

Alfie stared in awe, he quickly sat up and jumped out of bed. He slowly picked up the multi-coloured stone and the colours started to fade, along with the map, leaving Alfie in darkness again. Alfie was taken aback by what had just happened. Could the gem be...? No surely not... But Alfie had to say that the gem in the attic must be... MAGIC!!!

The next day Alfie remembered what had occurred during the night before and decided to tell Bobby. And he too didn't believe the spectacle that Alfie had experienced. Suddenly Alfie remembered the voice in his head asking for something. Alfie arranged to meet up with Bobby. It had been an odd three days and he needed to tell someone he knew who he could trust. Alfie wasn't convinced that Bobby really believed him, but they decided to hide it... for now.

They hid the gem under a crack at the back of Alfie's Granny's house. So that way, they could easily take it out and put it back in again without being caught. Alfie told a lie to Bobby though. Instead of confessing that there was a voice in his head and making his best friend think he had gone barking mad, he decided to say that he didn't want it because it could be dangerous.

No one could know about the voice in the night.

No one would believe it.

Chapter Five

The Spread

The next day Granny went to her mantelpiece to stare in pride at her artwork that she likes to make. Every Wednesday, Granny made clay figures in a shed at the bottom of her garden. Sometimes the figures were playing a game, or two clay figures were hugging each other - it was Granny's hobby. Sometimes when Alfie was very well behaved, Granny would make a clay model for him to take home. Alfie was outside playing football when he accidentally fell over; his knee hurt a bit, but he dusted himself off and carried on.

Alfie regularly went to football training and recently won the tournament; Alfie had the trophy on his bedroom shelf at home. As he was coming back inside, he was thinking about home and Mum and Dad. He was beginning to miss them greatly.

Meanwhile, Granny popped upstairs into the loft to see if she had any old ornaments that had been discarded or forgotten about that she could sell, as her clay modelling group were doing a fundraiser. She noticed that the silver box had been opened. Due to Alfie's carelessness of not closing the lid before taking the gem away, Granny would soon be asking questions.

Granny went downstairs and asked, *"Alfie, Sweetheart, did you take anything from the loft yesterday?"* Alfie started to confess and tell Granny that he took a gem. *"Oh, that old thing!"* Granny chuckled. Alfie let out a sigh of relief. Then Alfie decided to ask how she ended up finding the gem, why she kept it and why was it in the loft.

She started *"60 years ago ..."*

"I went out to play on my new toy rocking horse. At the time, rocking horses were all the craze and were adored by kids all over England. My mother and father had saved up their money and bought one for my birthday.

She was a 'Rocking Rose' with a white mane and brown leather harness.

Suddenly something in the corner of my eye appeared to glow, coming from underneath the grass. Curious as any nine year old would be, I scratched at the dirt with my fingers where the light was coming from and that's when I found it... the gem!"

Alfie asked if he could keep it and she said he could because she didn't know what it was, and to be honest her story was so long ago she wasn't even sure if it'd actually happened or whether it was just the imagination of a child. But something told her to keep it all these years.

And then she warned him that around the same time she found it, she started having strange dreams, nightmares even, about a voice asking for a gemstone? She assured him though, this was just the wild imagination of a child.

* * *

Meanwhile … In Movalwar

Mendoviolent paced the room, slamming his hands on his table in anger.

"I am running out of patience; I have made it clear what I have requested!"

"And now he shall suffer, the world will suffer!"

"TROOPS!" he commanded.

"Send more of the virus - more parasites!"

"For as long as that world has my gemstone, they will continue to perish."

"Some have died, but the message obviously isn't strong enough - increase the strength of the virus immediately!"

Chapter Six

The Bronze Papered Legend

That night Alfie lay down in his bed. For no reason at all, he felt more sleepy than normal, and soon drifted off to sleep as his curtains swayed and danced in the cool evening breeze. There was a silence in the air that fell like a dark blanket. Something was going on outside.

Outside in the cold night air, the gemstone in the crack was glowing... RED; something big was happening! In the house Alfie started to feel the headaches coming on again, and he knew what was about to happen, but this time he sat up for it and listened intently.

"You have disobeyed me greatly; I have asked for the gemstone AND I SHALL GET IT!" Alfie was shocked! It wasn't this loud when it spoke to him before. "You are running out of options, the people around you are becoming sick! Continue and there will soon be no one left."

Alfie sat and panicked at this threat. Mum and Dad were having tests... Trevor was really sick... Somehow, he knew that the voice was sending the virus to Earth. But how?

And then it was gone...

Alfie pondered over everything...the voice, the gemstone, the map, the virus...

That night it was clear that Alfie wasn't going to sleep; he stayed up wondering what to do. He decided he could not do this alone and decided to come clean to Bobby. He needed some advice.

In the morning, Alfie explained to Bobby everything that had been happening, and said that he needed some guidance.

"I have something that might make it clearer for us both of us," said Bobby.

"Oh really?" questioned Alfie, a little confused

Then Bobby revealed it all...

Bobby said that in his attic at home he found a book years ago. *"It was like a story book, but I didn't ever think it could be real,"* he said. *"Anyway,"* he excitedly carried on ...

"In the book, the paper was in fact bronze, and it told of

a legend that once there was a magical gem that could be put into a boulder, by a hidden lake, where there was a little slot for it to go. It was called 'The Switch', and could change surroundings forever."

"There was also an evil god called Mendoviolent who had been searching the galaxies for hundreds of years for the gem, when in fact the gem was here on Earth! And he wanted it so that he could destroy the gem, therefore keeping the kingdom in its evil state forever."

It was all so clear to Alfie now; the voice was Mendoviolent!

And Alfie had THE GEM... If he didn't give it back, Mendoviolent might kill everyone on the planet - including Mum and Dad.

Chapter Seven

The Depths

Alfie knew what he had to do - he needed to get to Mendoviolent somehow, so that he wouldn't take thousands of innocent lives! But first he needed to call upon his best friend Bobby, he had decided that he would never be able to do any of it without him.

They hatched a plan. They both waited until late at night when Granny was asleep and when Bobby's parents were asleep too. The streetlamps were glowing and the night sky loomed over them; Bobby and Alfie snuck out of their houses. They planned to meet up were the gem was hidden and decided to go from there.

"Hey," said Alfie.

"is it still there?" asked Bobby eagerly. It was, and Alfie didn't hesitate to pick it up. *"What now?"* said Bobby. Alfie explained that the last time he held the gem it started to glow. *"Well make it do it again!"* Bobby was almost shouting by this point.

"Calm down, Bobby" insisted Alfie. Bobby suggested rubbing it. *"It not a magic lamp,"* said Alfie, rolling his eyes. He tried it anyway as he didn't have a better

idea. Bobby gave Alfie a smug look, and suddenly colours shot out of the gem and projected a map onto the fence at the back of the garden. There it was again - the map!!

Upon closer inspection, it led far out of town. *"Right, are you ready for this?"* said Alfie, and that was when they set out on a wild adventure!!!

The boys were a little afraid because they didn't know where they were going. They had the map for directions, but they didn't know where they would end up. Soon they came to a fence with barbed wire spiraled around the top. *"Is this where we need to go? Do we need to climb over?"* said Alfie. The map was pointing past the fence.

"But there's nothing but sticky mud and reeds over there, mate," said Bobby confused.

"Do you want to go first?" whispered Alfie hesitantly.

So, Bobby and Alfie took their turns climbing the fence. When Alfie jumped down, he landed feet first into the sticky mud. Bobby wasn't kidding when he mentioned the sticky mud, it almost filled his socks.

The pair plodded along until Bobby shouted to Alfie, *"Stop!"* They were at their destination. *"But there's nothing here!"* said Alfie, annoyed at the situation.

But Bobby was right!

There was a lake next to them and the moonlight shone into the water and showed that there was something down there. Without thinking, Alfie jumped in.

"ALFIE, WHY DID YOU DO THAT? You'll be soaked for the walk home," said Bobby. And yes, Alfie would be wet and cold on the way home, but right now the most important thing to him was investigating the light down there.

Somehow, they needed to swim down to the bottom to see what it was.

Alfie and Bobby were members of a swimming club and therefore were very good swimmers. Without the swimming club, Alfie and Bobby wouldn't be the great friends that they were.

"There's no chance we're getting down there, we're not in

our swimming gear," said Bobby, *"and it looks deep; we might need a snorkel so we can get in and look down to see how far down it is,"* pointed out Bobby.

It looked as if they would need to come back with the proper gear. Alfie was frustrated that the night's plans seemed to have been put on hold.

"Come on Bobby, we'll just have to make do, were not at swimming training now."

Bobby jumped in. *"Argh, its freezing!"* Bobby shivered.

"Keep moving, you'll soon warm up," Alfie muttered.

Moving around in the lake so much seemed like a good idea until Alfie felt something move inside his pocket. *"Oh, no!! the gemstone... it's slipping out of my pocket"*. Just then the entire lake began to glow. *"Woah, what's happening"* Alfie said.

"It's the gemstone," said Bobby, *it's reacting with the lake."*

Soon it was so bright that neither of them could open their eyes. Bobby shouted, " We'll have to swim down Alfie, we can't lose the gemstone!" They both took a huge breath and plunged their heads into the water.

The pair swam and swam and swam. Both of their swimming skills were put to the test as they desperately held onto their breath because they were so far under, that if they opened their mouths, it would be their last. Alfie was closing in on the gem; he tried to catch it but it merely slipped through his fingers. He was starting to become tired; it felt as if the lake just went...

Down.

Down.

Down.

Forever.

Bottomless.

Just then he caught it and felt a great sense of relief. If only he could breathe a sigh of relief! Alfie noticed that Bobby was waving his arms around, he was pointing to something in the darkness.

Alfie was torn between coming up for air or going to

investigate. He quickly swam over to Bobby and was astonished to see a circular rock, and in the middle of it, the water started to ripple. It was almost like a window.

Then it dawned on Alfie. It was a portal...

Bobby decided to swim in first and waved at him to join him. They went in and just like that they were gone...

Chapter Eight

Enter Mendoviolent

Everything - the sky, the water, everything - was gone! Alfie turned around; Bobby was still there.

"Where are we?" said Bobby. It appeared they were floating, as if they were still in water, only different.

"I think we're stuck here, Alfie," Bobby said.

"What about Granny, and Mum and Dad?"

Would he make it out of there alive? He might be trapped.

Would he ever see them all again?

Alfie started to cry but knew he couldn't cry in front of Bobby, so he hid his tears.

Suddenly the ground began to shake and a massive white explosion blinded their eyes. They both fell to the ground with a thump. Unconscious.

A few moments later...

Alfie woke up, dazed, his face was in what appeared to be moss. Something was crawling on his face, tickling his skin as it moved. Disgusted, Alfie bolted upright. The bug before him was like a millipede but for some reason it was purple. Just then the bug bit Alfie on the cheek.

"Arghhh!" he wailed in pain, as he immediately swiped it off his face. It scurried away and dug into the mossy floor, disappearing. Alfie felt the spot where it had bitten him, it was already swollen and stung. He looked around for Bobby.

"Alfie, where are we?" He was about to answer Bobby when he was interrupted... A bellowing voice boomed in their ears.

"I SEE YOU HAVE COME TO RETURN WHAT IS RIGHTFULLY MINE!" It was Mendoviolent.

For the first time Mendoviolent and Alfie locked eyes. He was a dark, eerie, Viking-type figure that hid himself under a dark cape. *"AND I SEE YOU HAVE BROUGHT AN ACCOMPLICE."* Bobby's head spun to glance worriedly at Alfie. There was a deadly silence. From the darkness, a boney, old hand covered in war wounds and scars reached out towards him.

"GIVE IT TO ME." He said. Bobby looked as though he wanted to speak but he froze with his eyes about to pop out of his head. Alfie found the courage to respond, *"Actually I've come to make this land what it was before you reigned and caused pain and suffering."*

Mendoviolent responded, *"You know what they say - you cannot change the past!"*

Alfie paused, *"No, but you can change the future."*

"ENOUGH CHEEK, BOY! YOU WILL PAY. TROOPS, SEIZE THEM!"

The hand drew back into the darkness and two eyes shone brightly, though his face was still hidden in the shadows.

"RUN, BOBBY!" Alfie screamed! Mendoviolent summoned his men and the chase began.

They ran and ran, ducking and diving to dodge their arrows. They flew, almost skimming their heads as they ran.

"Alfie, look!" Bobby pointed. *"A cave!"* Hopefully some sort of protection; it had lots of high rocks, so they

took shelter in there, covering the entrance with a big boulder. Both boys were struggling to breathe, neither had ran so fast in their lives.

Panting, Bobby said, *"What is going on Alfie? Why did the gem choose us? We're such ordinary people, we're not special in any way."*

"I have no idea, all I know is that we cannot give him the gem, we have to fix this once and for all. Did you see all of those people around us? They're obviously scared of him"

Bobby nodded.

'What must Mum and Dad be thinking?' Alfie knew all too well that Granny and Grandad would be worrying so much. 'They'll have no idea where we are,' he thought. There was silence, although it was broken by a voice in the distance commanding,

"FIND THEM, I NEED MY GEM BACK."

The boys huddled up, Alfie slamming his hand over Bobby's mouth as he gasped. They were still out there looking for the boys.

That reminded Bobby. *"Alfie?" "Yes, mate." "Have you still got the gem in your pocket?"*

He fumbled around in his pockets...

"Bobby... It's not there!"

Chapter Nine

London's Struggle

Channel 4, London - BREAKING NEWS:

Two local boys, Bobby Wicket and Alfie Peterson, have now been missing for three days.

The grandparents say the last time Alfie was seen was when he was put to bed by his Grandmother, Joyce, on Tuesday night. Bobby was last seen eating his tea before going upstairs, his mother reports. When it was Bobby's bedtime, she came upstairs and shouted to ask if Bobby was ok. She got no reply and carried on walking up the stairs only to find that Bobby was not in his bedroom, but his bedroom window was open.

Both of the boys' bicycles were missing, but no clothing was taken from their rooms. It is thought that they have met up, but their whereabouts are unknown.

Two images of the boys flashed up on the screen.

Both boys are 11years old.

Alfie is thought to be wearing a green t-shirt, jeans, and an old 'Beavers' cap, he is around 4 feet 10 inches.

Bobby is thought to be wearing a white top with a blue hoodie jacket with shorts, height 4 feet 6 inches.

Please contact the Police on 0203 446 7149 if you have any information.

The broadcast continued...

... a local man who was out walking his dog late at night, gave an interview saying he heard the voices of two young boys shouting by the lake at the back of his house. Police have searched the area but have not found any items of clothing; however, they did find two bikes matching the description of those belonging to the boys.

More information to be released soon.

In other news ...

The virus pandemic has reached its peak with more than 20,000 people dead. Scientists have not known of this type of virus since medieval times and no cure has been found. Health advisors are saying that everyone in London should be wearing face masks to stop the infection rate going up.

It is very important we all follow the rules and help to stop the virus. You must not meet your family or friends to avoid getting the virus or them getting it from you.

Make sure that children stay inside because children are more at risk than adults.

We have no idea what is causing this virus and are still to create a vaccine. Scientists are clueless as to what to try next, as tests have been carried out for weeks now. The rate of infection is rising, and the side effects are... Well... strange to say the least.

Please stay away from anyone you think may have it as this is highly infectious.

If social distancing rules are not met by the public, then you WILL be arrested by the police.

If you own a shop and you are struggling to earn money, please contact your bank and they can give you a bank loan of between £500 to £1,000.

Remember, we are all in this together, so if you are having problems coping or struggling to remain positive, it is best to ring your doctor and speak to them about your worries over the phone.

With that, the news reader began to scratch his head, he looked hot, his face began to turn a deep shade of red, his eyes turning yellow...

He stopped reading and mouthed the word, "HELP!"

The news cut off with a long beeeeeep.

Chapter Ten

Alex

ondon had been plunged into chaos with people stealing from shops to survive. Homes had been vandalised and boarded up, with people not going outside anymore. The streets had become a hunting ground. The residents had gone crazy because nothing had changed since the day the virus started...

And then it all started overnight.

A big, black cloud loomed over London and red lightning struck the roads and eventually struck the people. One by one the streets were cleared; people lay dead on the roads and that was just the start. This was no longer classed as a virus... it was an invasion. Posters with the words 'MISSING' written across the top covered the streets of London, and there was an eerie silence.

* * *

Meanwhile ... Back in Movalwar

Alfie and Bobby had to leave the cave because Mendoviolent's troops came in search of them. They came so close, but the boys kept very still and quiet until they passed by.

The boys believed the safest thing to do; was to keep moving. That way, the troops wouldn't find them. The pair took it in turns to find food and each took turns sleeping at night whilst the other kept an eye out.

The food was weird though. Alfie's favorite was the occasional little blue mushrooms they would forage; to Alfie they had a distinct crunch and flavorsome taste. Bobby's favorite were the small green fish, the pair would walk to a little spot where they knew there was a lake and tried to grab some as they swam by. The only problem was that the fish were fast swimmers, and the only way to gain the prize was to corner them. This meant the boys would sometimes need to fish together.

They were sitting by the lake when Bobby asked, *"Alfie are we ever going to make it out of here?"* In all honesty, Alfie wasn't sure; without the gem, how could they get back through the portal?

But little did they know that their luck was about to change.

They both jumped and spun around when they heard a rustling noise in the bushes behind them. Eyes wide open, they were about to ditch their catch for the day and make a run for it when all of a sudden, a small figure appeared. A boy. About their age, a little younger maybe. He looked messy, dirty, so much so that they couldn't tell what colour his hair was. Alfie and Bobby weren't sure if they could trust the local village boy, until they both saw the pain in his eyes.

"Hi," he whispered *"My name is Alex. Don't be afraid, I'm here to help you."* Alfie and Bobby took a slight pause and looked at him blankly. *"Please!"* he begged. *"There's not much time."*

They decided that they were too visible should the troops pass by, so dashed to the hidden spot that the boys had made their home a few days earlier.

They sat down, *"Look, Alex, if you're going to be helping us, we need to know where you came from and how you're going to help us."*

Alex nodded... *"Five years ago Movalwar was a nice city of hope; birds and tropical wildlife flourished and spread like a wildfire - until Mendoviolent came and ruined everything. He used the gem to activate 'The Switch' which turned these lands into what you see today."*

"Five years?" Alfie questioned Alex. *"How can it be five years? My Granny has had this gem for like 50 years!"*

"I think we've gone into another dimension Alfie, not just travelled to a different world, but a different time too!" suggested Bobby.

Alex continued. *"The only people who eat properly are Mendoviolent's troops. The rest of us are just his slaves."* Alex looked as though he was about to cry. Alfie threw a quick glace over at Bobby. Alex continued...

"They were struck with red lightning - my parents, I mean. I remember their faces as they looked at me for the last time before they lay lifeless on the floor. I ran and ran and have been taking care of myself ever since. I remember my Dad showing me something very special. He told me that one day I'd need it and that I'd know what to do... but I didn't have a clue what he meant."

"What?" asked Alfie

Alex reached into the tatty backpack he'd hidden under a blanket that was tied around his shoulder and pulled out a sword! It was short, maybe more of a dagger. But it glistened. Easily the shiniest thing that the boys had ever seen. It seemed to glow once Alex passed it over to Alfie.

"See… my Dad was right. I knew I'd made the right decision to come to you," Alex said with a smile. He went on to explain that he believed the sword could kill Mendoviolent, turning the kingdom back to how it was before.

"Use the gem, turn it back into the kingdom it used to be then kill Mendoviolent once and for all!" Alex urged them.

Then he said… *"And that's why you need my help, I've got a plan!"*

Chapter Eleven

A Dangerous Plan

*A*lfie said, *"Right, how are we going to kill Mendoviolent?"*

"Well, we need to get up close to him to kill him with the sword," said Alex.

"Is there anything else in this magical world that could possibly kill him?" worried Bobby.

"You're not going to like this, but I'll say it anyway, ermm no," Alex said sadly. *"If you want to kill Mendoviolent, you have to use this sword to do it."*

"Great!" Sighed Alfie, sarcastically, not feeling very sure about this situation at all.

"Oh, by the way, there may also be another problem... we lost the gem," Alfie confessed. The boys expected Alex to be disappointed that the *'grand plan'* couldn't go ahead. But instead he just smiled. He looked down and opened his hand to reveal the precious... GEM! The boys couldn't believe their eyes, and felt a mixture of relief, shock and confusion.

"I've been trying to find you both for a few days and came across it whilst near that big cave by the lake."

"WELL DONE!" shouted Bobby with glee.

"Shush Bobby, the troops may hear us," said Alex; so they all whispered *"yay!"* in hushed voices. For the first time in days, Alfie and Bobby had a reason to smile. They might even get back home after all.

Alfie was now desperate to get a plan together. *"Hey, what if we creep up on him?"*

"So out of all the great ideas that COULD work, you decide to creep up on the Master of the Dark Arts?" said Alex, unimpressed.

"Actually it might just work," said Bobby.

"Ok, this is the plan," said Alfie. *"I will take the sword because I am the tallest, and therefore have the better chance of killing him."* Alfie did a little measure with his hands and he was right. *"I will creep up on him from behind,"* said Alfie.

"But you can't do it all by yourself," said Bobby.

"That's where you come in. Bobby, you will be our lookout; you have to constantly check if any troops are nearby. If there are troops nearby, you will give me and

Alex a thumbs down; if it's clear, you give us both a thumbs up. Got it?" explained Alfie.

"Yes, Sir!" said Bobby, another sarcastic face.

"What about me?" said Alex as he looked excited to know what his job would be.

"You Alex, will be our bait."

"BAIT!" said Alex in disbelief. *"Do I look like bait to you?"*

"What fine bait you are," said Bobby, happy that he wasn't bait.

"Ok," said Alex reluctantly. *"But I propose an idea."*

"Go on," said Alfie and Bobby in unison.

"If we want this to work, then we need to test it out, no?" said Alex.

"Yes! Amazing! We will try it out on this Aldara," he said, pointing towards a nearby tree. An Aldara is an ancient bird that hunts down prey and only lives in Movalwar.

Alfie had once read about them in a library, only they were classed as a mythical creature. Clearly not mythical after all! A few stupid and clumsy attempts later, thinking they could simply grab an Aldara from the tree...

"Shush," said Bobby *"... it's right there."* One lone Aldara landed near Alex. *"Keep still, Alex,"* whispered Alfie. Alex, otherwise known as bait, dashed out and waved his arms at the bird. Alfie saw his chance and swung the sword just as it was about to bite and inject its purple venom into Alex's leg. It's said that the venom can take weeks to kill its victim, slowly turning them completely purple, unable to move, then frozen in time forever and as cold as stone.

SLICE! Alfie had slain the mythical creature. Purple blood splattered the ground.

The plan had worked on a particularly fast and vicious bird... Maybe it could work on Mendoviolent?

Either that or they would die trying and fail miserably.

No one knew for sure...

Chapter Twelve

Death

Alfie's eyes flickered open. He woke up thinking it was his Mum waking him for school, but he quickly remembered he was trapped in another dimension with no way out but to kill an evil king. The dream ended quickly. Looking up at the inside of the cold, brown, wet cave his smile disappeared. *"Great,"* he muttered to himself and since he was awake, he decided that the others should be too so walked over and gave them each a little shake.

"Hey, why did you wake me up?" asked Alex angrily.

"Yeah, me too?" said Bobby.

"Remember guys... a little matter of killing Mendoviolent?" said Alfie.

"Oh yeah... that!" said Bobby with a sigh. Alfie stood, pacing whilst Bobby and Alex yawned, and rubbed their eyes.

Alfie said, *"Do we have everything?"*

"We do," said Alex.

They had the sword to kill him with, they had the gem

to change the kingdom back, the plan and the bait. But first they needed to find Mendoviolent and that was going to be very easy - just follow his troops back to their castle. Within the next few minutes, they quickly packed up what belongings they had gathered, grabbed a few snacks and off they went.

Sooner than they expected, they heard some of Mendoviolent's troops talking amongst themselves. They were shocked to know that they had been so close, especially as the three boys had been sleeping just moments ago. The troops were saying it was a waste of time continuing the search and that we were probably long gone by now! They followed the troops back to the castle, making sure to keep a good distance away, never speaking and only communicating with hand gestures.

The three boys crouched down behind a hill, peering through the leaves. Beyond the hill, about 300 meters, was a dark throne, surrounded by huge rocks the size of houses. There he was - Mendoviolent - giving orders and getting servants to do his bidding!

"GO!" he bellowed. The troops did as they were told, leaving Mendoviolent alone.

This was their chance. Alex began to creep forward. *"Where are you going, Alex?"*

"Now's our chance I'm going to distract him but listen, if I don't see you both again, then I want to say 'good luck'. If I'm captured, he'll definitely double the troops to look for you... after killing me," he gulped. *"Bait, remember?"* With that, he ran, still crouching down.

Bobby and Alfie stood up to watch Alex running, hoping and praying this would actually work. He made it, he was now stood right in front of Mendoviolent. Alex seemed smaller, tiny even, as Mendoviolent rose up and towered over him. They locked eyes.

Alex found the courage to speak. *"Why did you destroy the kingdom all those years ago? All those lives lost!"*

Mendoviolent seemed to smirk but it was hard to tell. *"I HAVE NEVER HAD ANYTHING IN MY LIFETIME. I HAVE NEVER OWNED ANYTHING; I WAS A SCAVENGER*

UNTIL I LEARNED MAGIC. THAT WAS THE ONLY THING I HAD!" bellowed Mendoviolent.

"ONCE I WAS THE MASTER OF DARK ARTS I DECIDED TO KILL EVERYONE THAT TOLD ME I WAS NOTHING." He continued, *"NOW THEY ARE AFRAID OF ME AND THEY SHOULD BE! I'M FINALLY TAKING WHAT IS MINE."*

"But why did you kill my parents?" asked Alex with sadness in his eyes.

"THEY, AS MANY OTHERS DID, TRIED TO STOP ME. NO ONE IS A MATCH FOR ME. THEY FELL AS EASILY AS THE LEAVES FROM THE TREES!" He let out an evil laugh and seemed to gesture to someone to come over.

It was clear that Alex's idea of a distraction meant striking up conversation. But before the conversation went any further, Alex was approached by two men and grabbed. He was waving his arms around, trying to wriggle free.

Alfie and Bobby both gasped and glanced at each other. *"Now"* Alfie said. The boys took one step forward but just then two servants leapt out of the bushes and grabbed at their ankles. They looked demented, robotic, as if under the control of something, or someone!

They tried hard to fight back, kicking and lashing out. Alfie punched at the chest of one, and with a gulp he dropped Alfie. Bobby was still squirming. The servant grabbed at Alfie for a second time and his long, slender arms swung into his face, making Alfie feel weak and nauseous. Alfie was face to face with him, and for the first time he realised that he wasn't a regular servant or even a part of the troops. He seemed infected, almost like a creature, obviously under Mendoviolent's control.

The creature opened his mouth only for Alfie to see another creature inside about to launch out towards Alfie to eat him; but he had had just about enough of this and found some strength from somewhere. He wriggled enough to be able to reach the sword and swung it wildly. It had sliced his arm. Alfie immediately fell to the ground. Bobby's creature dropped him and ran after seeing the sword. The boys both lay on the ground panting for air, staring at the one-armed creature laying on the ground.

His chest started to squirm and a lump moved around his dead body, and then the creature crawled out of the wound and scurried away.

They took a moment to catch their breath but, as they stood up, they realised they were surrounded. The last thing they saw were two servants approaching them with a baton and then they blacked out.

* * *

Alfie was coming around, his eyes constantly opening and closing until they were forced open. They were in a room, in a cage. Mendoviolent was at the other end of the room and they were being guarded by troops. Glancing over, Alex was there too.

"Psst... Alex," he whispered.

Alex gave a weak smile. *"Looks like we have met again after all."*

"Time to give being bait another go," Bobby said, pointing to a guard standing nearby.

"Ok," said Alex with a deep breath. He slid his arm through the metal bars and grabbed a rock then threw it at the servant, causing him to stumble and fall.

"HEY YOU! OVER THERE! PULL YOURSELF TOGETHER, OR I WILL KILL YOU, SERVANTS *DO NOT FALL OVER!"* ordered Mendoviolent. As the servant stumbled, Alex reached out and grabbed a key for the cage. He quietly opened it and scrambled over to Bobby and Alfie.

It was now or never, before someone noticed that they had escaped.

"Charge!!!" shouted Alex. They all ran forward, shoving servants out of the way until they reached the throne. Alex and Bobby continued forward as Alfie separated off and ran into the shadows. Mendoviolent stood, towering above them.

"YOU CAN NEVER DEFEAT ME!"

"No, but he can..." Bobby panted and smiled an evil grin.

Alfie appeared from the shadows and stabbed Mendoviolent in the chest.

"*NOOOOOOO!*" he wailed, gasping for air. Mendoviolent's eyes glowed bright yellow before he burst into a thousand pieces. The boys fell to the ground covering their eyes to shield the blinding light. There was whooshing and crashing noises all around them.

When the noises stopped, the boys dared to open their eyes and stand back up.

Everything was different.

Lighter. Prettier.

No evil,

No Troops,

and...

No Mendoviolent!

Chapter Thirteen

Rejoice

Alex took the boys to 'The Switch' which was hidden beneath mossy rocks and dead earth, deep in the heart of the forest they could see the orb and the slot for the gem to be placed into, but it was guarded by vines that stretched across like fingers.

Alfie approached slowly and pulled back the strong vines.

He was about to put his hand inside the orb, when suddenly the gem vibrated and made a high-pitched hum that created a shock wave throughout the forest. Then, as if magnetised, the gem leapt out of his hand into the slot.

Alfie and Bobby squinted at the light it produced, then slowly opened their eyes. The legends were true! The world was blossoming with life all around them. The bug on the floor that tried to bite Alfie had turned into a bright and colorful caterpillar that started to crawl onto a nearby tree. Parrots swooped over their heads and the air was filled with sounds of crickets chirping and the soothing sound of waterfalls in the distance. And most of all, the once evil troops were now transformed into civilized and well-meaning men and women who at once tried to rebuild houses for themselves to live in. All the while monkeys played and swung in the trees above.

It would take years of renovation, but all were determined and had hope in their hearts to restore what was once theirs before they were deceived by Mendoviolent.

"We did it. We actually did it!" cheered Alfie. All of a sudden, the townspeople cheered, and all the animals cheered too. The sound of elephants filled the air, the monkeys screeched along with the birds and the tigers roared as if they were cheering too! A voice from the crowd shouted *"YOU'RE OUR SAVIOURS."* It was the townspeople; they surrounded the boys with smiling faces, clapping.

"Here, take this as a token of our gratitude." Two men walked up to the boys and placed crowns of roses and violets on top of their heads. *"Please stay here as long as you like. We would all be very grateful if you..."* He paused and looked sheepish.

"What's wrong?" asked Bobby.

"We would love it if you maybe stayed, forever?"

"Thank you," said Alfie with a smile, *"but our families will be missing us."* All of the townspeople sighed but understood. They were just grateful to have freedom and live surrounded by beautiful nature again.

The boys turned to face Alex, stood at the edge of the crowd.

"I'm sorry," said Alex. *"But this is where we must part ways."*

Bobby looked confused. *"But you helped us defeat Mendoviolent and his troops? You could come back home with us!"*

Alex didn't ponder the thought for a second. *"Ah, yes I did, but my family are buried here and as much as you are good friends to me, I would rather part ways with some friends than with my family."* He made a good argument.

"Alright, Alex if it makes you happier, we understand."

Just as this was said, the gem flew out of Alfie's pocket and crashed into the lush grass, a portal was created, then it flew back into Alfie's hand.

"That's us, then," Alfie said nodding towards the portal. *"Are you sure you don't want to come back to Earth with us?"*

"I am quite sure," said Alex, *"but thank you... for everything."*

The villagers shouted and roared as they walked into the portal...

WOOOOOSSHHHHH!!!

They were thrown out on the other side of the portal, a little dizzy, but had to get their bearings quickly in the water. It was impossible to see each other through the murky water and thousands of bubbles. They vigorously kicked their legs and scooped the water with their hands.

They quickly swam to the edge of the lake and rested on the bank. It was only then that they realized how cold they were - it was a freezing evening. Shivering and dripping wet, they took a moment to catch their breath which was visible with white smokey clouds.

Placing the sword and the gem on the grass, Alfie stuttered through the cold...

"Bobs... We just saved the world!"

Chapter Fourteen

Peace

B obby panted, *"So where do we go from here now?"*

"We don't have Alex anymore to tell us what to do next, he was a brilliant friend who helped us do something that we couldn't have done by ourselves," grimaced Bobby sadly.

"I know it's hard, but you always have to pull through," said Alfie as they started to walk down the path near the highway. *"I guess now we go home and try to explain all of this, somehow?"*

As they were walking, dripping as they went, they noticed that the once speeding cars were nowhere to be seen. They presumed that it must be really late and that's why it was so quiet.

Just then something came flying down the path in the distance but with moonlight bouncing off it. *"What on earth is that?"* said Bobby squinting. Suddenly it came and smacked Bobby's face. It was just a newspaper. After all of the crazy things they'd witnessed recently, it was a relief for it to be something so normal.

Alfie grabbed it off Bobby's face laughing. Then the headline caught his eye. Still walking, Alfie read the newspaper aloud. It read that there had been a virus spreading and killing London citizens. It seemed serious. As panic washed over them they realized that they had no idea if their families were safe.

"No", cried Bobby. They didn't speak as they looked at each other for a moment, both thinking the same. With that they began to run, feeling heavy under their wet clothes. They ran past houses that were boarded up and some even partly demolished with signs saying:

'Enter at own risk'.

'Danger'.

Or scariest of all ...

'Infected - Do not cross the line!'

They reached the road that they both lived on and parted ways after agreeing to meet back up in one hour, whatever the outcome was to be at home. Alfie had the sword and Bobby had the gem.

Alfie ran, feeling the water squelch in this trainers. What would he do if Mum and Dad were gone? He pushed the thought from his mind as he caught sight of the blue front door with a dead plant pot outside. Home. He noticed it too had boarded-up windows as he knocked on the door quietly.

KNOCK, KNOCK! He listened through the door and looked through the keyhole. Nothing. Inside looked different. Everything had been piled up against the windows, from what he could make out. He knocked again.

"It's me, Alfie, are you home, Mum?" He whispered. There was a short pause, *"Dad, you there?"*

He stood up and turned around, looking down the road then back at the house. He was about to go to Bobby's house but just then the door opened with a creak.

"ALFIE, WHERE *HAVE YOU BEEN?!"* said a voice. It was Mum! She had a look of desperation, sadness and amazement all at once but with love in her eyes. She looked as though she might cry.

"ALFIE, AWW MY SPECIAL LITTLE GUY, YOU'RE HOME!" she reached out her arms.

After Mum had calmed down and Dad was told the good news too, they sat down on the sofa and Alfie told them everything. Their faces looked as though they didn't quite believe him. Why would they? It was crazy.

"But..." Mum said, trying to think of the right question. Alfie cut her off...

"And that's when he gave me this to kill him with," he said, as he pulled out the sword as proof.

Frankly, Mum and Dad were gobsmacked, especially when Bobby and his parents turned up on the doorstep with the same story! Together they all spoke, looked at the sword and the gem, asked questions; the boys explained all they could. Eventually, they believed them.

Dad insisted that they should destroy the gem once and for all. They all agreed.

Alfie and Bobby quickly dried off, threw on some

clean clothes, then made their way immediately to the secret lake, that wasn't so secret now.

"It's time to end this, all the madness, confusion, scariness, all of it forever," said Alfie.

He placed the gem on a nearby rock, took a tight grip of the sword and swung... 3... 2... CRACK!

Just then the ground began to shake, and the lake burst with blue light, and it flickered and dashed towards the city.

The crumbling buildings were restored, all the lost family members rose back to life, the crumbling chunks of road were fixed, the upturned cars were returned to their wheels and the fires that covered them were put out. It was as if someone had hit the rewind button. The blue light shattered and sprinkled across the city, raining down.

Balance was restored and what a sight it was! The gem lay on the ground - shattered and cracked open. Bobby took a step forward and gathered the pieces of the once solid gem, and forcefully tossed them into the lake - the pieces making little ripples in the water as they disappeared beneath the surface.

Alfie's Mum put an arm around him and so did Dad as if they were watching a firework display. Alfie took a brief glance at Bobby - his Mum was doing the same to him.

Peace was made in Movalwar. Never to be altered again. Alex could live a happier life, knowing his parents didn't die in vain.

London was saved. The virus ended.

And the adventure drew to a close... or so they thought.

THE END

About the Author

Hello, I'm Benjamin Cornelius, but my friends call me Ben. I love books. They can take you on a journey and that's what I've tried to do in my book, 'Movalwar'.

I have been inspired by the books that I have read including Ollie Locke's 'Islands of Fandye'. I was taken aback by how magical and wondrous books can be. They really take you on an adventure, no matter if you are 11 years old like me or older. You can still have an adventure when reading, no matter your age.

I have also taken inspiration from TV shows such as Netflix's 'Stranger Things'; I loved the magical element of that show.

This is the first book that I have ever written. I wrote it during the 2020 global pandemic when I was in lock-down with my family. Boredom has struck many and that is why I have chosen to write this book. I hope you enjoy reading this as much as I have enjoyed writing and designing it.